S0-DON-550

SEWER SQUAD!

Based on the teleplay "Metalhead" by Tom Alvarado

Illustrated by Jacob Chabot

A GOLDEN BOOK • NEW YORK

© 2013 Viacom International Inc. and Viacom Overseas Holdings C.V. All rights reserved. Published in the United States by Golden Books, an imprint of Random House Children's Books, a division of Random House, Inc., 1745 Broadway, New York, NY 10019, and in Canada by Random House of Canada Limited, Toronto. Golden Books, A Golden Book, and the G colophon are registered trademarks of Random House, Inc. Nickelodeon, Teenage Mutant Ninja Turtles, and all related titles, logos, and characters are trademarks of Viacom International Inc. and Viacom Overseas Holdings C.V. *Turtles to the Rescue!* previously published in slightly different form by Golden Books in 2012. Based on characters created by Peter Laird and Kevin Eastman.

ISBN: 978-0-307-98226-1

randomhouse.com/kids

MANUFACTURED IN CHINA

10 9 8 7 6 5 4 3 2 1

The Teenage Mutant Ninja Turtles!

Leonardo leads with steel!

© Viacom International Inc.

Michelangelo's *nunchucks* take care of business!

Raphael gets a kick out of fighting crime!

© Viacom International Inc.

Donatello battles with his brains and his *bo* staff!

The Turtles emerge from the sewers to fight crime.

© Viacom International Inc.

The Kraang attack!

Let the battle begin!

© Viacom International Inc.

"Chuck this out!" says Michelangelo.

"How am I supposed to fight alien technology with this stick?" asks Donatello.

© Viacom International Inc.

Later that night, using an old Kraang-droid, Donatello builds a new weapon.

Meet the future of *ninjutsu*–Metalhead!

© Viacom International Inc.

Raphael is not impressed.
He wants to do his own fighting.

Donatello's robot has some awesome moves.

© Viacom International Inc.

Nighttime brings another mission.

Donatello stays in the lair, controlling Metalhead—and eating pizza.

© Viacom International Inc.

Metalhead is strong, but he's also slow and loud.

In the Kraang's warehouse, the Turtles overhear a plan to infect the city's water supply with mutagen.

© Viacom International Inc.

The Turtles drop in for a surprise attack!

"This is epic!" says Raphael.

© Viacom International Inc.

The Kraang blast Metalhead!

Metalhead is damaged—and out of control!

© Viacom International Inc.

Donatello races to help his brothers.

"Time for some Turtle teamwork!" says Donatello.

© Viacom International Inc.

Metalhead meets his maker.

Metalhead is no match for Donatello's staff.

© Viacom International Inc.

KABOOM! Metalhead is destroyed—and so are the Kraang's barrels of mutagen.

Donatello's staff breaks, but he stops
Metalhead—and the Kraang's evil plan!

© Viacom International Inc.

Victory tastes like pizza!

"Thank you, Splinter," Donatello says. "With a new staff and proper training, anything is possible."

© Viacom International Inc.

Turtle Power!

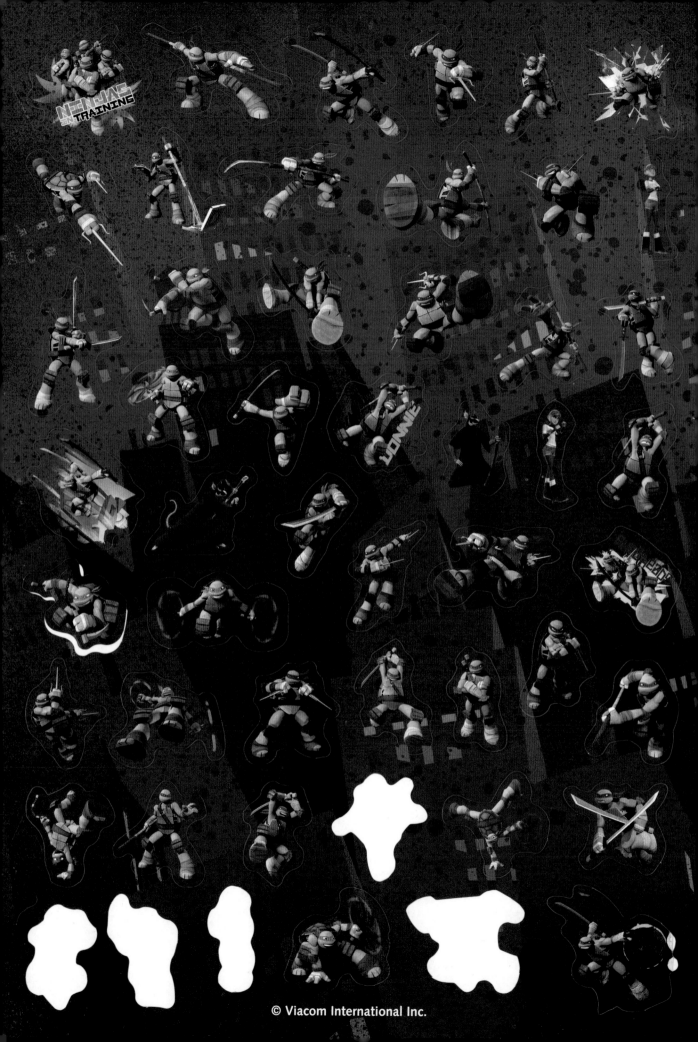

© Viacom International Inc.

© Viacom International Inc.

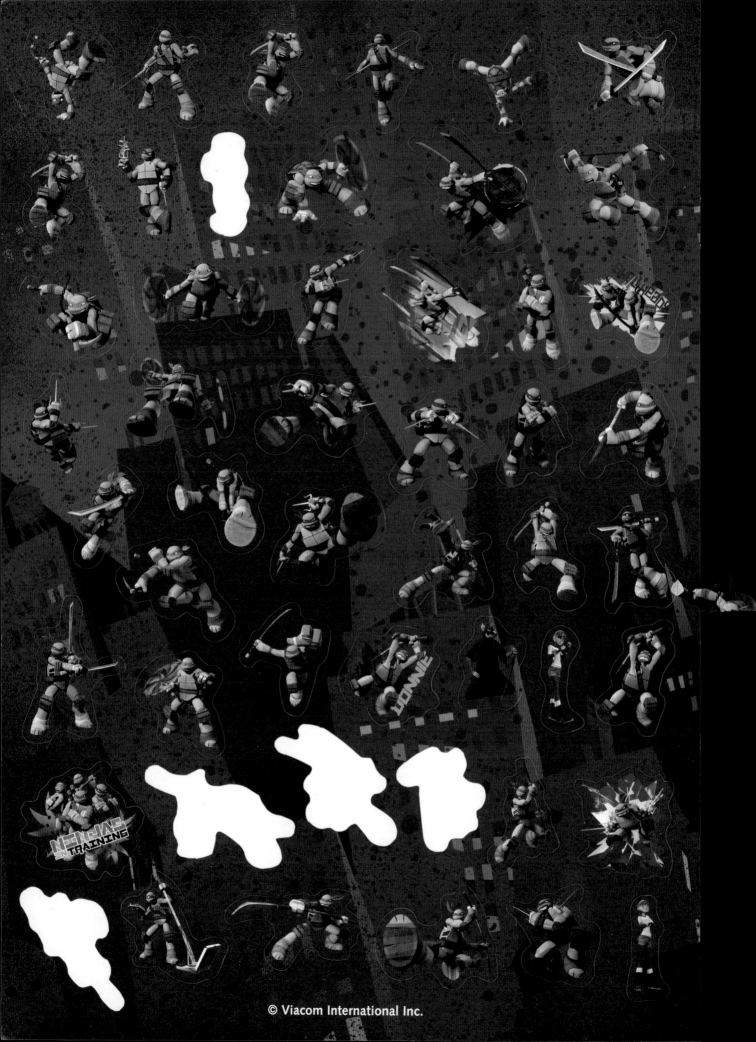

© Viacom International Inc.

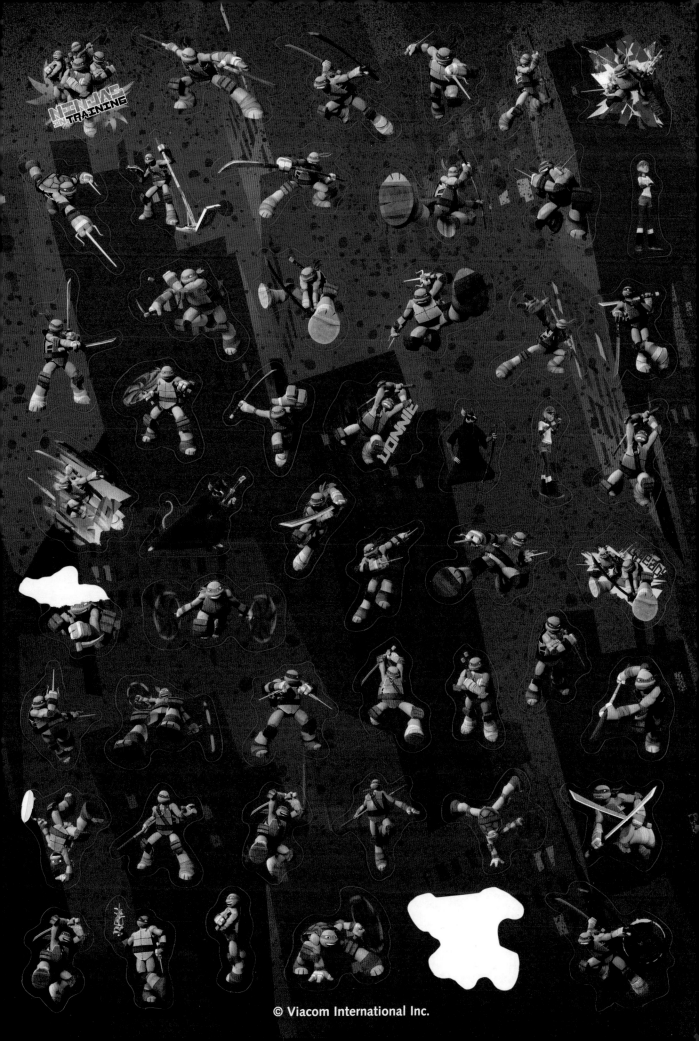

© Viacom International Inc.

© Viacom International Inc.

nickelodeon™
TEENAGE MUTANT NINJA TURTLES™

TURTLES TO THE RESCUE!

Based on the teleplay "Day One, Parts One and Two"
by Joshua Sternin and Jeffrey Ventimilia

Illustrated by Shane L. Johnson

Welcome to the streets of New York City.

The city is filled with adventure—and pizza!

© Viacom International Inc.

The Turtles interrupt a crime.

© Viacom International Inc.

The Turtles aren't very good at teamwork.

Michelangelo discovers that the bad guys are really robots with weird alien brains inside!

© Viacom International Inc.

The bad guys get away—with the girl and her father!

Back in the lair, Splinter says, "Your inability to work together allowed the bad guys to get away."

© Viacom International Inc.

No one believes Michelangelo's stories about robots and alien brains.

Splinter knows the Turtles need a leader.

To see who he chooses, slowly tilt the page
away from you and read the name.

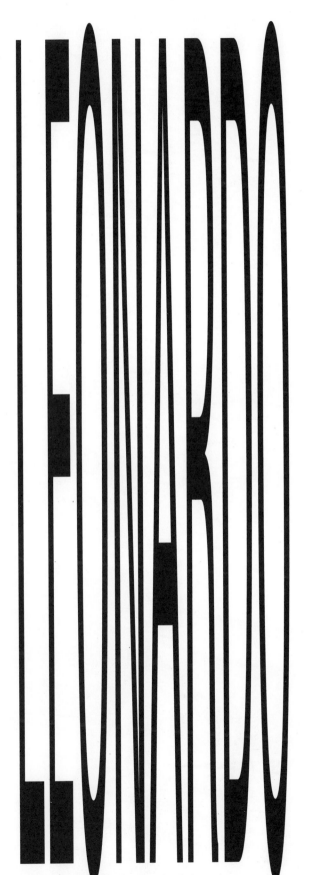

© Viacom International Inc.

ANSWER: Leonardo.

The Turtles return to the city streets.
"We've got to save that girl," says Leonardo.

"That building has the same logo as the van we're looking for," says Leonardo.

Help the Turtles find the van.

START

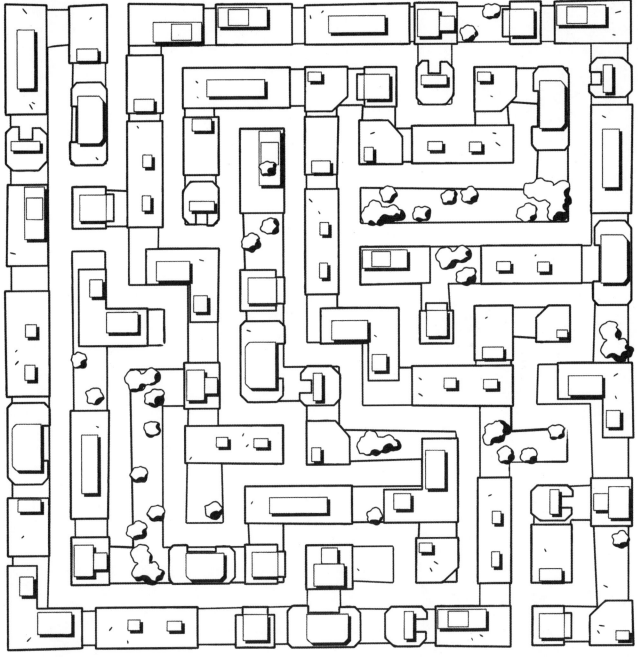

FINISH

© Viacom International Inc.

ANSWER:

The Turtles stop the van.
It's filled with the chemical that mutated them!

The Turtles have some questions
for Snake, the driver of the van.

© Viacom International Inc.

Snake tells the Turtles who the bad guys are.

Use the key to learn the name of their evil organization.

R	N	H	E	A	G	T	K

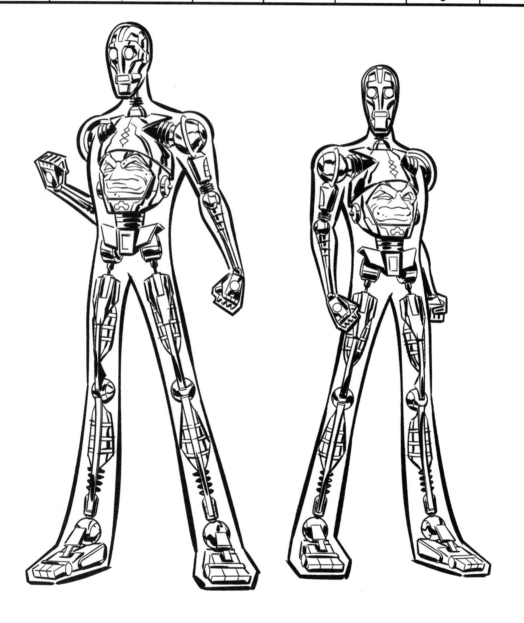

"We should storm the Kraang's factory now!" says Raphael.
"It will be an all-you-can-beat buffet!"

"We can't just rush in," says Leonardo.
"We need a plan!"

© Viacom International Inc.

"We'll go back to the lair and gear up," says Leonardo. "Then we'll use Snake's van to sneak into the Kraang's factory."

Snake, who is hiding nearby,
hears everything.

© Viacom International Inc.

That night, a van races toward the Kraang's factory.

Snake has warned the Kraang that the Turtles are coming.
They are ready and waiting!

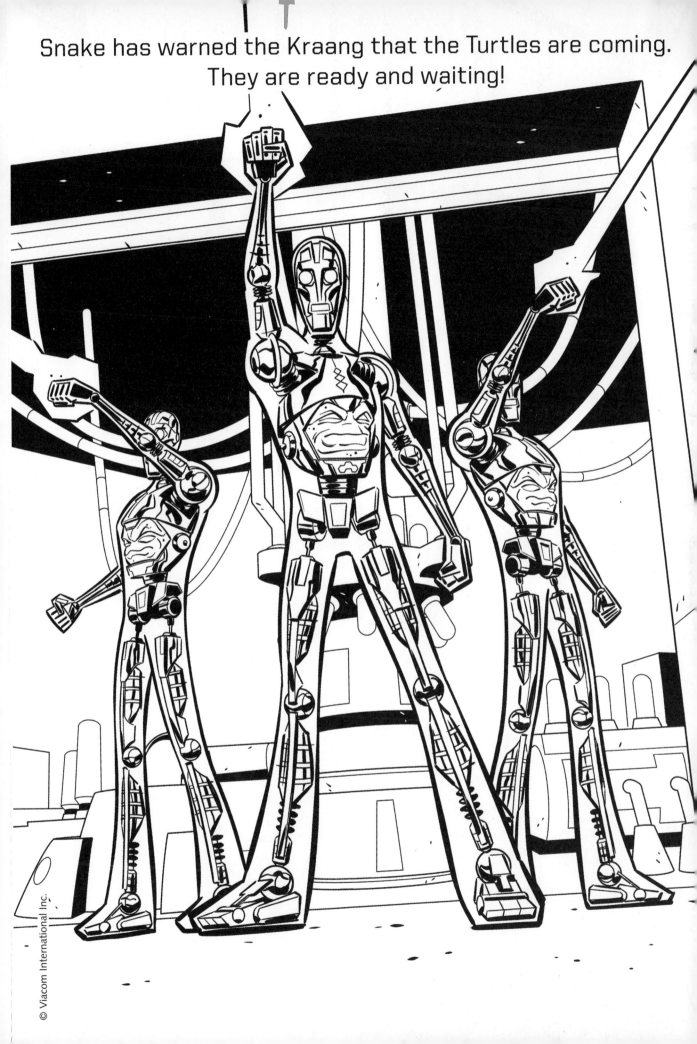

© Viacom International Inc.

But the Turtles aren't in the van!
They knew Snake was listening and are
sneaking into the Kraang's base another way.

Leonardo and Raphael battle the Kraang—
and make an amazing discovery!

© Viacom International Inc.

"See, I told you," shouts Michelangelo.
"I was totally right about these brain things!"

Help Donatello find the girl and her father and lead them to Leonardo.

START

© Viacom International Inc.

ANSWER:

FINISH

Snake is splashed with the secret
chemical—and turns into a giant weed!

"You'd think he would have changed into a snake," Michelangelo says.

© Viacom International Inc.

The Turtles and the girl, April, escape on a helicopter—but April's father is left behind.

Back at the lair, Splinter tells Leonardo that he is very impressed. "You proved to be an effective leader," he says.

© Viacom International Inc.

April vows to find her father—and
the Turtles promise to help her!